WELCOME TO

Beast Quest

Collect the special coins in this book.
You will earn one gold coin for
every chapter you read.

Once you have finished all the chapters,
find out what to do with your gold coins at
the back of the book.

With special thanks to Tabitha Jones

For Taylor and Kasey Anderson

www.beastquest.co.uk

ORCHARD BOOKS

First published in Great Britain in 2018 by The Watts Publishing Group

1 3 5 7 9 10 8 6 4 2

Text © 2018 Beast Quest Limited.
Cover and inside illustrations by Steve Sims
© Beast Quest Limited 2018

Beast Quest is a registered trademark of Beast Quest Limited
Series created by Beast Quest Limited, London

A CIP catalogue record for this book is available from the British Library.

ISBN 978 1 40834 339 5

Printed in Great Britain

The paper and board used in this book are made from wood from responsible sources

Orchard Books
An imprint of Hachette Children's Group
Part of The Watts Publishing Group Limited
Carmelite House, 50 Victoria Embankment, London EC4Y 0DZ

An Hachette UK Company
www.hachette.co.uk
www.hachettechildrens.co.uk

Beast Quest ®

JuroG
HAMMER OF THE
JUNGLE

BY ADAM BLADE

ORCHARD

CONTENTS

Quake before me, Avantians. You think you are safe in your distant kingdom, but you couldn't be more wrong.

All of Makai is under my control. This island's ancient Beasts are risen again and obey my every word. The people are my slaves, building a force unlike any you've ever seen. I will do what my mother, Kensa, and my father, Sanpao, never could...I will have vengeance on Tom and his people.

You can muster your soldiers. You can assemble your navy. But you will never be ready.

I'll be seeing you very soon.

Your soon-to-be ruler,

Ria

TROPICAL STORM

Tom's stomach lurched as the flying dinghy listed sharply with a sudden updraft, pitching him against its wooden rail. In a jumble of limbs, Elenna slid down the bench and slammed into his side. The forested hills of Makai swam sickeningly far below. *If we tip any further we're going to capsize!*

"Lean right!" he told Elenna. She grabbed the rail on her side of the boat. Tom braced his muscles and shifted his weight towards her. The boat levelled and he let out a breath of relief.

"Flying's...even...worse...than sailing..." Daltec panted, his face greyish green as he frowned back at them from his seat at the bow.

"It's this boat!" Tom grunted, both hands on the wooden tiller, trying to hold it steady. "I don't think it was meant for strong winds or long flights."

Tom, Elenna and Daltec had taken the flying boat from the Elixir Wells, where their pirate enemy Ria had been mining the floating fuel to power her flying ships. As well as defeating Larnak the Swarming Menace, Tom and his friends had managed to drain away much of the floating elixir in the wells before escaping. Unfortunately, Tom suspected that Ria had already mined enough to launch an attack on Avantia from the sky. Their only hope now was to stop Ria building her magical ships. *But somehow, we'll have to find her first...*

"We're heading for a storm," Elenna said, pointing. Ahead, the scattered clouds of Makai drew together, casting deep shadows over the jungle below. Even as Tom

watched, the dark clouds thickened
and swelled, rolling across the sky.

Tom clenched his teeth. "Just
what we need!" He closed his eyes
to summon the strength from his
golden breastplate, which was part
of his Golden Armour. The suit stood
on display back in King Hugo's
palace, but Tom could call on its
magic wherever he was. He heaved at
the tiller, trying to steer the dinghy
around the angry-looking bank of
cloud. But at the same moment, a
strong wind slammed into the keel,
making the craft judder. The sunlight
darkened to a murky brown and a
curtain of rain spread down from
the clouds ahead. Forked lightning

crackled across the sky, followed by
a rumble of thunder.

Suddenly, the boat pitched. Tom
clung to the gunwale with one
hand to stop himself falling against

Elenna. Daltec whimpered.

The gloom deepened. A rush of heavy rain hit Tom's face. He braced his arms, using every muscle to keep the tiller steady, but mighty gusts tore at his body, straining his grip, driving the boat ever closer to the heart of the storm.

"Hold on!" Tom cried as the boat tipped suddenly forwards, making his stomach drop away. Another gust righted the dinghy, slamming Tom back on to the bench. Elenna crashed down, half on top of him, then slid back into her seat. Rain pelted them from every direction.

"Aargh!" The tiny dinghy rolled hard to the right, tearing his hand from the tiller. The craft began to spin, faster by the moment, whirling like water down a drain.

"Brace yourselves!" Tom called. "We're going to crash!" He crouched low, hugging the deck. At his side Elenna did the same.

Pop! Silence rang in Tom's ears as the buffeting wind and driving rain stopped. *No…* Tom could still see the rain lashing down as they spun, but somehow it didn't reach them. A faint blueish glow surrounded their boat. At the bow, Daltec now sat upright, chanting under his breath. *He's created a force field!* The wizard's body trembled and the sinews stood out on his arms with the effort of working his spell.

"He won't be able to hold the force field for long!" Elenna said.

Tom heaved at the tiller, finally managing to bring the boat out of its downwards spin. *Crack!* A sizzling flash of white exploded in his vision. Daltec let out a cry, and the glowing bubble surrounding their boat flickered. Then it popped, sending a shower of fizzing sparks cascading downwards.

All at once the rain and wind hit with full force. A forked tongue of lightning hit the keel. *No!* Tom's chest tightened with horror as he saw purple elixir flowing from a hole burned in the wood, leaving a glittering trail behind them. His stomach leapt into his mouth as they plummeted, losing height fast, the boat's prow angled downwards,

cutting through the storm towards the ground.

Tom threw up his shield, calling on the power of Arcta's eagle feather to slow their fall. He felt himself lift from his seat and grabbed the slick wood of the bench with his free hand. The weight of the boat almost tore Tom's arms from their sockets. Using the magical strength of his breastplate, he braced his arms between his shield and the boat... But still they sped towards the treetops below.

"The boat's too heavy – we'll have to jump!" Tom cried.

"No! We'll break our legs, or worse!" Daltec shouted.

"I can heal broken bones," Tom said. "But I can't bring us back to life. Jump! Now!"

"No!" Daltec cried. "I've got a better plan." Tom saw his friend wave one hand, tracing a bright rune in the air, then flick his fingers towards the ground, sending a stream of fizzing blue energy bolts down through the tree canopy. "Hold on tight!" Daltec cried, throwing himself down inside the boat as they plummeted.

AMBUSH

Tom held his shield before his face as branches whipped past. Twigs scratched his skin and snagged his clothes and hair. Crash after crash filled his ears. Half-darkness greeted him as they shot through the canopy. *I hope Daltec's spell worked!* Tom thought, wincing...

SPLASH!

Warm water swirled around him as the dinghy plunged keel-first into darkness. Bubbles streamed past his face and his ears popped. He kicked himself free of the boat and pumped his legs, silt and weed clinging to him as he pushed for the surface.

Finally, he broke out into the stormy shade of the jungle to see they had landed in a small, perfectly circular pool. Heavy raindrops plopped down into the water all around him and the treetops roared with the wind. Tom laughed. *Daltec magicked up a pond!*

Elenna broke the surface a moment later, spluttering, her wet hair plastered to her head. Daltec

emerged beside her. He blinked
the mud from his eyes, spat out
a mouthful of water, then started
for the bank of the pool. Tom and
Elenna followed.

"You could have conjured up a cleaner landing!" Tom said, as he staggered towards Daltec, squelchy mud sucking at his boots and filthy water streaming from his sodden clothes.

"That would have been preferable, I agree," Daltec said, squeezing brown water from the hem of his tunic, "but I was in a bit of a hurry."

Elenna grinned. "Tom's only teasing. I'm not sure we'd have survived at all without your quick thinking!"

Tom led his companions further into the rain-lashed forest. The air was hot and thick, with barely a breath of wind reaching the ground.

Bowed beneath the weight of their sodden clothes, they pushed in single file through leafy ferns and hanging vines. Where the foliage grew too thick, Tom used his sword to clear a path, but in the stifling heat, his weapon soon felt heavy.

As they pressed on, the rumble of thunder grew distant, and the rain gradually petered out. Shafts of sunlight slanted down from above, and water vapour rose from the glossy foliage all around them.

"At this rate we'll never catch Ria!" Tom growled. They plodded on as fast as they could through the sweltering jungle until the trees suddenly thinned. Tom pushed through a curtain of hairy, grey vines and found himself in a clearing scattered with circular wooden huts. Elderly men and women with crinkled, sun-browned skin and greying hair sat at the entrances to

many of the huts, tending small fires or grinding grain. A bow-legged man looked up, scowling, and Tom noticed that one of his eyes was misted white. The man rose and hobbled towards them, using a stick for support.

"Leave us be!" he spat. "There's no one left here who can even walk properly, let alone work."

Tom and Elenna exchanged a look. This was far too familiar. *Ria!* Tom thought. *She's enslaved people here too!*

Tom held up his hands. "We wish you no harm," he said.

"Then go away," the man said.

Tom nodded. "Come on," he said to Daltec and Elenna. "I've a feeling Ria might be closer than we thought."

As they left the village behind, the crackle of flames and the thud of pestle on mortar were quickly replaced by the steady chirp of cicadas and the harsh croak of frogs. Birds rustled in the treetops, letting out piping trills of song. The further they walked from the village, the more uneasy Tom felt. He found himself glancing back over his shoulder, as if something were watching them from the darkness – something that made his skin prickle and his nerves thrum. A muffled crack from the shadows caused him to spin, but not so much as a leaf trembled in the heavy air of the jungle behind them.

"Someone's following us," Tom hissed to Elenna and Daltec. At the same moment, he heard a soft whistle of air right by his ear. *THUD!*

Something pinged off the tree trunk beside him, leaving a white scar in the wood. Tom bent and picked up a small, flattened stone from the ground near the tree. As he turned to scan the jungle, another missile whizzed towards him. He batted it aside

with the flat of his sword. Elenna strung her bow, and peered into the undergrowth.

"Can you see anything?" Tom hissed. Elenna shook her head. *Ping!* Another stone rattled off a mossy rock near Elenna's feet. Tom ducked behind the broad tree trunk, gesturing for Daltec and Elenna to follow. *Thwack!* A stone slammed into the far side of it. Peering out from behind the tree, Elenna let an arrow fly, aiming in the direction the shot had come from. A thicket of ferns bobbed and rustled, then another, as if something scurried between them. Tom spotted a pair of skinny brown legs among the bobbing leaves, and pointed.

"Try and get behind those ferns," he told Elenna. "Wait for my signal, then charge!"

Tom stepped out from behind the tree and lifted his sword, scanning the foliage around them as if still searching for their attacker. "Come out!" he cried, swiping at a vine, hoping to cover the sound of Elenna's movements. He spotted her shadow slipping between the ferns ahead. Once he was sure Elenna was in place, he lifted his hand. "Now!" Tom charged headlong towards the swaying ferns while Elenna dived in from the side, her arms reaching low, towards the sun-browned legs.

"Ow! Get off!" a young voice

cried. As Tom passed through the feathery fronds, he found Elenna gripping tightly on to a sinewy boy who was squirming on the ground, a slingshot in one hand. Tom stepped lightly on the slingshot, pinning it to the jungle floor. The boy scowled up at him from fierce grey eyes half hidden beneath a thatch of dark hair. He wore a simple tunic, frayed and smeared with dirt, and looked to be around seven or eight.

"Why are you attacking us?" Tom asked the child.

"Because you're pirates!" the boy answered. Though his voice quavered with fear, his eyes shone with fury. "I'm not letting you capture anyone

else from my village."

"We're not pirates," Tom said, "and we won't hurt you or your friends."

The boy scowled. "I know a pirate when I see one. Only pirates walk around the jungle with steel blades."

Tom sheathed his sword and knelt slowly at the boy's side. "I promise you, we're not pirates. We've come all the way from Avantia, and we're here to fight the pirates. Do you know why they are taking the people from your village?"

Elenna loosened her grip on the boy, allowing him to scramble up to sitting.

The boy shrugged. "No," he said. "After they captured me, I managed to slip my feet from their manacles. I ran until I was sure they couldn't find me."

"Why didn't you go back to the village?" Elenna asked softly.

"They took my father!" the boy

answered. "I'm not going back without him."

"Brave words!" Tom said. "You sound like just the sort of boy that could help us with our Quest. What's your name?"

"Isaac," the boy answered. Then his eyes opened wide and he started. "Someone's coming!" he hissed. Tom listened, and heard footsteps crashing through the undergrowth, then a harsh, guttural laugh. "He'll be in here somewhere," a rough voice growled.

Isaac scrambled under Elenna's grip, his face drained of colour. "It's them!" he cried. "The pirates!"

RESCUE MISSION

Tom threw Isaac behind him
and shot to his feet, brandishing
his sword as three tattooed men
stepped from the undergrowth. He
charged straight for the biggest of
the three – a bald man with a thick
red beard and ice-blue eyes. Elenna
bent double and let out a scream,
bundling towards the middle pirate –

a short, fat man with an eyepatch.

Before the bearded pirate could even lift his whip, Tom leapt forwards. *CRACK!* He whacked the

man over the head with the butt of his sword. Beside Tom, Elenna drove her shoulder hard into the fat pirate's rounded gut.

"Oof!" The man doubled over, puffing and blowing. Elenna chopped him neatly over the back of the neck with the side of her hand. He staggered, then toppled forwards, crashing face-first into the dirt beside the pirate Tom had struck.

"Stay back!" Daltec cried. Tom spun to see his friend wielding a thick branch like a club as the last of the pirates – a lanky youth with greasy hair – lurched towards him, leather whip raised. Something whizzed past Tom's cheek. The pirate staggered back, blood trickling from a cut on his forehead.

"Got him!" Isaac cried. Daltec dived forward, swinging his branch with such force it splintered to fragments as it struck the lanky pirate's skull.

"Nice work, team!" Tom said, as the youth slumped to the ground beside his comrades. "Now we need to go and stop Ria and free the villagers – and thanks to these three ruffians, I have an idea."

A short while later, the three pirates lay on the ground, wearing nothing but their underclothes. Elenna grinned at Tom and spread her arms wide. "How do I look?" she asked, turning slowly. Tom wrinkled his nose. A filthy white shirt with a tattered lace ruff covered her tunic. She'd pulled a leather belt tight about her waist to hold up baggy trousers tucked into high, leather boots. A grimy bandanna hid her spiky hair, and she wore a leather eyepatch over one eye.

"You look as bad as I smell!" Tom said, glancing down at his own grubby pirate garb – a leather waistcoat and striped pantaloons that felt stiff with layers of dirt, and a blue neckerchief that stank of old socks and onions.

Daltec wore a open-necked shirt with flowing sleeves under a faded red waistcoat, and held one of the pirate whips in his hand. As he caught Tom watching him, the wizard twisted his face into an ugly leer. "Yar! What yer looking at, landlubber scum? I'll make ya walk the plank!"

Elenna giggled and shook her head. "You might just pass for a pirate if you don't open your mouth," she said. "That accent is terrible!"

Isaac, too small for the pirates' clothes, had tied a red sash round his waist, and covered his dark hair

with a striped handkerchief.

"Ready?" Tom asked, shoving an iron key into his pocket. Isaac had found it on one of the pirates and recognised it as the key to the villagers' manacles. The young boy lifted his slingshot with a grin. "Ready!" he said.

Elenna nodded. "Me too!"

Daltec shrugged. "As I'll ever be," he said.

Isaac led them deeper into the jungle. Apart from the occasional alarm call from a startled bird, Tom heard nothing. Before they had travelled far, he noticed broken twigs and crushed foliage in their path.

"People have passed this way

recently," he told the others.
"Hopefully the trail will lead us to
Ria."

The track of scuffed earth and
snapped branches widened as
they followed it. Soon Tom could
see bright sunlight slanting down
through a clearing in the tree canopy
ahead. The rich smell of soil filled
the muggy air. When they reached
the patch of sunlight, Tom stared
down into a huge dark hole ripped
in the forest floor, lined with hairy
roots. The sight sent a chilly finger
of dread down his spine. Daltec let
out a low whistle. "Something tore a
whole tree from the ground," he said.
"But what?"

"One guess," Elenna said.

"A Beast, clearly," Tom said. "But what kind?"

"There's another hole over here!" Isaac called. He'd scampered further along the trail. Tom trod carefully towards the boy, studying the soft earth of the forest floor as he went. He quickly spotted what he'd been looking for – deep, widely spaced claw marks. His gut tightened with worry.

"A huge one, by the looks of it," Elenna said, scanning the tracks.

Tom took the lead, his sword raised and senses sharpened by the adrenaline coursing through his veins. Above the steady beat of his heart, he could hear the distant thud of axes on wood. They passed more gaping holes in the forest floor.

Tom kept low, skirting between bushes and tree trunks, picking his way carefully around the craters. The thunk of axes grew louder. Before long, Tom could make out the crack of whips, and angry shouts and cries of pain. He pressed through a thicket of spiny bushes, then drew back, pity and fury swelling in his chest. He gestured to the others to stop.

Ahead lay a wide clearing, busy with activity. Workers with axes, their feet manacled and their tattered clothes soaked with sweat, clambered over fallen trees, hacking off branches and stripping away bark. Peering through the bushes, Tom could see girls and boys little older than infants working alongside adults almost as ancient-looking as Aduro. Pirates in grimy leathers

stalked among them, barking orders and cracking whips. A great stack of pale trunks, stripped of their bark, were piled on top of each other at the far side of the clearing. Another pile of trunks complete with roots and branches lay to the left.

"We have to free those people!" Elenna hissed, peeking through the foliage at Tom's side.

"I've counted ten pirates," Tom whispered. "That's three for each of us – if you can take down one with your sling," he added, turning to Isaac.

"I'll take down more than one!" the boy answered, his eyes burning with anger.

Tom held up a hand suddenly, listening. Over the sounds of axes and whips from the clearing he could hear the thump of running footsteps – heavy ones, getting closer by the moment, making the ground tremble. Elenna let out a groan as she and Tom watched the edge of the clearing, waiting, the branches around them shivering in time with the footsteps.

"I guess we're about to see whatever Beast yanked up those trees…" she muttered.

JUROG, HAMMER OF THE JUNGLE

Tom tightened his grip on his sword as a gigantic eight-limbed monkey crashed from the treeline into the clearing. The Beast stood upright on two bowed hairy legs, its head reaching almost to the tree canopy. Between two of its six muscled arms it cradled a whole tree, trailing roots.

Matted, purplish fur covered its body, everywhere apart from the leathery skin of its face, and of its six huge hands. The Beast glared down at the slaves in the clearing from crazed-looking pale eyes, a string of saliva hanging from the tip of one sharp white tooth. Ria's slaves glanced nervously at the monster, before quickly turning their eyes back to their work.

"Jurog!" Daltec hissed in Tom's ear. "One of the four ancient Beasts of Makai vanquished by the Masters of old. The legends refer to him as the Hammer of the Jungle because his tail is tipped with a redsteel mace."

Jurog carried the tree in his arms

to a huge pile of felled trunks waiting to be stripped of their branches. He tossed it as easily as if it had been a twig, then turned to stomp back into the jungle. Tom saw that Daltec was right. The creature's long, supple tail ended in a bulbous scarlet mace covered with lethal-looking spikes.

Once the Beast had gone, Tom scanned the lumberyard again, his mind racing to come up with a plan. "We need to get all these people out of harm's way," he said. He turned to Daltec. "Stay here with Isaac. Look after my sword and shield and lend me your whip – I don't want our weapons to give us away." Then he pulled the metal key from his pocket.

"Elenna and I will unlock the slaves and tell them to run when we give the signal."

Elenna passed her bow and quiver to Isaac, holding the boy's gaze gravely. "I'm trusting you to look after this," she said. The boy nodded, his eyes wide.

Tom rubbed a handful of dirt from the forest floor across his face, then tied his neckerchief around his head, covering one eye and half his face. He and Elenna waited for two thickset pirates with whips to stroll past, exchanged a nod, then swaggered into the clearing.

Tom stopped at the first group of workers that they came to – a huddle of four young women hacking the branches from a felled tree not far from where Daltec and Isaac hid.

"We're here to rescue you," Tom hissed. The women paused in their work to look at him, their weary eyes suddenly filled with hungry, desperate hope.

"How?" one woman asked. Her blonde hair was damp with sweat, and she looked grey with exhaustion.

"I'm going to unlock your manacles. But don't run until I give the signal."

The woman's eyes darted nervously towards the treeline. "But how will we escape the Beast?" she asked.

"We'll deal with Jurog," Tom said. The woman nodded. Tom dropped to his knees and started to unlock her bonds, while Elenna stood with her back to him, shielding him from view while she kept watch.

Once all four women were free, Tom and Elenna moved on to the next group of slaves, then the next, always keeping as far from the real pirates patrolling the lumberyards as they could.

"We're almost done!" Elenna said finally. "Just those few men over there left to unlock!" She pointed at half a dozen men who were splitting a long, white log into planks. The men had stripped to the waist and their skin shone with perspiration.

As Tom started towards the group,

he heard a familiar cackle from above. He glanced up to see a small flying boat sail from the forest to hover above the clearing. Ria stood near the prow of the boat, her green eyes flashing with spiteful glee as

she ran them over her slaves. Tom lowered his gaze quickly so that she couldn't see his face.

"Put some backbone into it, you lazy, good-for-nothing cockroaches!" Ria bellowed cheerfully. "If you don't get a move on with my wood, I'll conscript you for my Avantian invasion. A long flight on short rations followed by the battle of your lives! How would you like that, eh?" The chop and scrape of axes on wood picked up pace as all the workers did their best to hurry. Ria cupped her hands to her mouth and shouted loudly towards the jungle. "Jurog! More timber, now! I want a fleet that would make my father green with envy!" Tom could hear the distant stomp of the Beast's feet as the giant monkey tramped through the forest, followed by the cracking, wrenching sound of a tree being torn from the earth.

A clang from nearby drew Tom's attention and he looked over to see one of the manacled slaves swaying on his feet. The man's dark hair was plastered to his head with sweat, and his grey eyes were hazy and unfocussed. The axe he'd been holding lay on the ground beside him, and as Tom watched, the slave sank to his knees, his eyes rolling up in his head. Tom leapt to the man's side and shouldered him back to his feet.

"Slacking off on the job!" Ria shouted from above. "How dare he? Flog the sluggard!" Tom froze, his arm still supporting the half-conscious man.

"What are you waiting for?" Ria bellowed. Tom gently released the man, who let out a moan and slumped to the ground. All around him, the sound of chopping had ceased. Tom could feel everyone watching. *I can't hit an innocent man!* he thought. *But if I don't do something, our cover is blown!*

Ria let out a growl of frustration. "For all the gold in Gwildor, do it now, or I'll have Jurog tear your limbs off, one by one!"

A ROUGH RIDE

Tom stood frozen, staring at the fallen worker, his whip a leaden weight in his hand. Suddenly, he heard a twang. Something whizzed past him.

"Gah!" Ria yelled. "What's going on?" Tom looked up to see her flying dinghy rocking wildly, one of Elenna's arrows half-buried in its hull. Ria clung to the wooden rail, her green eyes flashing with fury as she tugged at the tiller, trying to steady her craft. Glancing back to where he'd left Daltec and Isaac, Tom saw the young boy scowling up

at Ria along the length of another arrow, Elenna's bow clasped in his hands.

"No one strikes my father!" Isaac cried. Tom let out a groan. He couldn't blame Isaac for protecting his father. But still, a terrible sinking feeling settled in his gut. *Things are about to get ugly...*

"Is that right?" Ria hissed, smiling sweetly as her eyes fell on the boy. Then she scowled. "Well, no stinking little urchin thwarts my plans!" Daltec tugged Isaac back into the shelter of the bushes. "Jurog!" Ria called in a high, singsong voice. "I have a job for you!" A loud whooping shriek echoed from the jungle, followed by the crack of branches and the rustle of leaves. High boughs at the edge of the clearing bucked and swayed as Jurog swung from the treetops, landing before Ria with an earth-shaking thud.

"A little bug needs crushing," Ria told the Beast. "And I know how much you like that sort of thing." The giant monkey lashed his mace-tipped tail against the ground, making it shudder, then let out a long, low growl, scanning the clearing with a hungry glint in his pale eyes. Ria's workers trembled under the Beast's gaze, their faces ashen and their eyes terrified.

"Over there," Ria said, pointing

towards the undergrowth which hid Isaac and Daltec. Jurog let out a snarl, then started off in a loping run on all eight limbs across the clearing.

Daltec and Isaac will never outrun the Beast! I have to help them!

As Jurog sped past, Tom drew back his long whip, then cracked it down hard on the monkey Beast's tail. Jurog snarled and turned, his eyes narrowing and his teeth bared as he scanned the clearing for his attacker.

Tom cracked his whip again, this time catching the huge monkey across one of his broad shoulders, leaving a red welt.

Jurog lifted his head and let out a screech of rage.

"What do you think you're doing?" Ria called. "Jurog's on our side!"

Tom ignored the pirate witch, and lashed his whip again, aiming for the Beast's face. One of Jurog's hands flashed out and snatched the end of the whip from the air, then yanked it downwards. Tom's arms jerked painfully and his feet left the ground. *Whoosh!* He landed on his belly as Jurog turned and scampered away, dragging him behind.

"Oof! Ouch! Aargh…" Trees whizzed past in a blur as Tom bounced and skidded along on his front, his arms stretched out before him. *At least I've diverted his attention from Isaac…* Tom thought, his body jolting painfully with each ridge, bump and root. *But now I need to work out how to defeat this Beast!*

A tree trunk loomed into Tom's view. He winced and braced himself… *BOOF!* He ricocheted off the trunk, gasping at the pain in his shoulder, but somehow kept hold of the whip. Calling on the strength of his golden breastplate, Tom bent his arms and tucked his legs up beneath him as he sped over the forest floor. He twisted, gritting his teeth, and with a burst of effort managed to get his legs braced out in front of his body. Tom spread his feet, digging in his heels. His feet ploughed ditches in the soft earth as he heaved on the whip, trying with all his magical strength to slow Jurog's frantic pace.

Tom fell to the ground as Jurog

came to a sudden stop. The Beast
glanced back over his shoulder,
and as his orange eyes locked
with Tom's, they filled with mad,
animal rage. Tom stood up, his
mouth turning dry. *If only I had*

my sword... Jurog let out a howl of fury, then bounded towards Tom, his tail lashing wildly behind him, smashing tree trunks and leaving splintered gashes in the wood.

Tom's heart felt as if it might burst from his chest as the furious mass of muscle, fur and clawed limbs hurtled towards him, but he stood his ground. At the last possible moment, Tom called on the power of his golden boots and bent his knees. He leapt, soaring right over Jurog's head. Tom stumbled as he landed, then raced on. The Beast's thunderous footsteps quickly joined his own. Tom could feel the ground trembling with each step. He plunged onwards, leaping tree roots, ferns and jagged rocks. The crashing of falling trees rang out behind him, along with the pounding boom of Jurog's feet.

Tom's lungs burned and his legs felt rubbery with effort, but still he could hear the vast eight-limbed monkey gaining. The earth leapt with the Beast's mighty steps, making Tom stagger as he ran. A shadow fell across him from behind. Tom's heart clenched. *He's going to catch me!* Tom scanned the undergrowth frantically, looking for any escape. His eyes fell on a thick, glossy bush to his left. He flung himself into it, scrabbling with his arms and legs, pushing himself through the scraping, snatching twigs.

As soon as he was free of the branches, Tom spotted a steep incline covered in fallen leaves. A ditch lay at the bottom, partly overshadowed by the gnarled roots of a tree. He dived and rolled down the bank. Wriggling sideways, he wedged himself into darkness, forcing his body under the twisted roots, right up against the soil. He lay, sweat pouring off him, trying to breathe quietly, his lungs shuddering for air. He could hear loud snaps and cracks nearby – the sound of the Beast rummaging in the bush he'd

scrambled through. A series of loud, frustrated hoots pierced the air. Angry stomping feet paced this way and that...then Tom heard the creak of a branch, followed by the rustle of twigs and leaves far above. And finally, silence.

Tom lay for a few moments, catching his breath. *That was far too close...* Then he squeezed from his hiding place, and crept back the way he'd come. *Jurog's gone!* But even as Tom's body sagged with relief, a whooshing sound made him spin. Terror fizzed through his body. A bright red shining mace covered with long, sharp spines swung through the trees, right towards his face.

1

6

BATTLE BENEATH
THE BRANCHES

Tom threw himself headlong into
the dirt, then rolled, hearing Jurog's
spiked mace swoop over his head.
He sprang up, scanning the swaying
treetops, but Jurog had snatched his
tail back. Dense leaves and tightly
thatched branches hid the Beast
from view.

A chattering laugh echoed down from above. Leaves fluttered to the ground. As Tom pressed his back to the bark of a tree, his mind racing for a plan, he heard running footsteps.

Tom turned to peer out from his hiding place, and relief flooded his veins. *Elenna!* His friend jogged through the jungle, panting heavily, her hair plastered to her head with sweat. She'd taken off her pirate garb and Tom could see his sword shoved through her belt, and his shield slung over her shoulder. She held her bow and arrow ready in her hands as she scanned the treetops above. Leaves rustled. Elenna aimed upwards towards the branches that hid the Beast, and fired.

Tom heard the dull thwack of an arrow hitting flesh, followed by a howl of pain. Elenna fired another arrow, then another. Tom saw the branches of a tree ahead bend and sway, then another, further off. *The Beast's retreating!*

Tom stepped out before Elenna. "Thank you!" he said. "I really thought I was finished!"

Elenna rested her hands on her knees, gasping for breath. "I tracked you as quickly as I could," she said, "but that monkey's fast. Luckily, your trail wasn't hard to follow."

Tom rubbed his aching shoulder

and winced. "Tell me about it. I made it with my body!" Tom shrugged off his pirate clothes and tore the bandanna from his head. "Phew!" he said as a breath of air reached his sweaty skin.

Elenna handed Tom his sword and shield. "We'd better get going," she said. "Somehow, we need to defeat that monkey Beast. And that's before we can even think about facing Ria and her men."

Together they edged into the trees after Jurog.

Before they had travelled far, Tom heard a swish that made his guts twist with fear. He spun to see Jurog's tail swiping towards Elenna. *No, you don't!* Tom shoved Elenna aside and

swung his sword for the Beast's
hairy tail, but the Beast whipped
it up out of reach. Elenna steadied

herself against a tree, aimed her bow and let an arrow fly. Tom heard another fleshy *thunk*, followed by a furious scream.

"Good shot!" he told Elenna, grinning. "If we can keep this up, we might be able to wear that monster down!"

CRASH! Jurog dropped from the trees before them, making the ground judder violently, throwing Tom and Elenna off their feet. He landed in a twisted heap, a gnarled root stabbing into his back. Elenna hit the earth beside him, her head cracking against a stone.

The giant monkey Beast grinned down at Tom, a mad glint lighting his eyes as he lifted his spiked mace high. Elenna let out a moan, and Jurog's grin broadened as his eyes fell on her stricken form. Tom scrambled to his knees beside his friend, threw up his shield and braced his muscles.

BOOM! Pain exploded along the length of Tom's arms and his shield clattered to the ground. Terror burned though him, dulling his pain and sharpening his reactions. He tugged Elenna to her feet and thrust her out of the path of Jurog's glinting red mace.

CRASH! The spiked mace slammed into a tree, splintering wood, leaving a gaping hole. A

hideous creaking sound echoed from
the wounded trunk. Tom watched in
horror as the top half of the mighty

tree listed, then toppled...straight towards Elenna.

7

BLIND RAGE VS BRUTE FORCE

"Look out!" Tom cried. Time seemed to slow to a hideous crawl as Elenna started to rise, the falling tree casting a deep shadow across her back. Tom felt sick with helpless horror as he watched his friend glance up, her eyes opening wide as she registered the dense tangle of branches crashing her way. He didn't make it in time, and watched Elenna disappear under the weight of foliage.

Icy shock jolted through Tom's body. *No!* A painful lump filled his throat as he lurched towards the spot where Elenna lay hidden.

"RAAAWWR!" Jurog stepped into Tom's path, swinging a massive open-handed blow towards his chest, gnarled yellow claws spread wide.

Tom's blood boiled with rage. He let out a fierce cry and swung his sword, slashing it deep into the Beast's hairy wrist. Jurog snarled and snatched back his hand, then slammed two more vast leathery fists towards Tom like giant mallets.

Tom leapt, and spun, his sword lifted high. He felt his blade rake the flesh of one hairy arm then the other, sending a shower of red droplets cascading down. Tom landed in a crouch, then, spurred by fury and fear for his friend, he launched himself even higher, aiming his blade at the monster's broad chest. Tom's sword bit deep into Jurog's body and lodged there. The monkey Beast lifted his head and let out a wild screech of pain, then swiped for Tom with a fist. Before the blow could land, Tom yanked his sword free, and with both feet, pushed off Jurog's chest in a backwards roll.

Landing neatly, feet spread in a fighting stance, Tom drew his sword back ready to strike once more. Jurog glared down at him, his mouth stretched into a hideous rictus of fury. Blood oozed from the wound in his chest. Tom met the giant monkey's gaze, his jaw set, and the blade in his hand stained dark red. Jurog held Tom's eyes for a long moment, then let out a snarl and turned to lope away into the jungle. The Beast's eyes had held a clear message. *Jurog might be injured, but he'll be back...*

Tom raced to where Elenna lay beneath the fallen tree, his legs suddenly trembling with fear.

He clawed through the tangled branches until he saw her, half hidden beneath a thick bough that had landed right across her chest. "I'm…all right," Elenna said weakly, her words coming in gasps. "I'm trapped. I think I've broken a rib, but I'll live."

Dizzy relief flooded Tom's veins. He let out a shaky breath, then called on his magical strength. "I'm going to lift the tree," he told Elenna. "Do you think you can wriggle clear?"

Elenna nodded. Tom planted his feet wide, and, putting his hands either side of the vast trunk, bent his knees, and heaved. The strain

made his blood pound in his head
and his arms burn, but the tree
lifted fraction by fraction. Tom
puffed and blew, keeping the tree
raised until Elenna scrambled away
with a wince of pain. Then he let the

tree fall back to earth with a crash.

"Thank you," Elenna said, clutching her ribs. Tom took the green jewel from his shield. Elenna moved her hand and Tom held the green stone to the injury. Elenna's strained breath eased. "That's better!" she said. Then she took her bow from her back and gazed in the direction the Beast had run, frowning. "But how on earth are we going to beat that thing?" she asked.

"I think we need to draw Jurog out into the open," Tom said. "As long as he can lash at us from the treetops with his tail, we don't stand a chance."

Tom and Elenna started off side

by side. They saw no trace of the giant monkey as they skirted from trunk to trunk, except for the occasional gaping hole in the forest floor. Eventually they reached a small clearing pitted with craters where almost all the trees had gone.

"This might do," Tom said. But even as the words left his mouth, he heard a cracking, tearing sound from somewhere nearby in the jungle.

CRASH! The earth juddered, throwing Tom into the air. He landed hard on his back. Elenna crumpled to the ground at his side. Glancing up, Tom saw a vast tree trunk embedded like a spear deep in the ground right before them. He started to rise, but with another *CRASH!* a second trunk drove down into the earth beside the first.

Tom staggered up, the jungle floor shaking beneath him. Elenna scrambled to her feet beside him. They lurched away from the two huge trees to see Jurog emerge from the jungle carrying three more giant trunks, each drawn back ready for him to throw.

BOOM! CRASH! THUD!

The trunks sank deep into the ground with such force that earth and grit and splinters exploded into Tom's face, blinding him. *What's he doing?* Jurog let out a roar, ripping

two more mighty trees up from the
clearing's edge.

THUD! BOOM!

Tree after tree rained down,

closing off Tom's view and cutting out the light. The ground beneath Tom quaked so hard it felt as if it might open up and swallow him whole. When the shaking finally stopped and silence fell, Tom rose and gazed around in the half-darkness to see their escape completely blocked. Tree trunks stood side by side all around them, forming a tight, impenetrable ring. Jurog let out a whooping howl of triumph followed by a long, chattering laugh.

"So much for fighting out in the open..." Elenna said quietly.

ALL OR NOTHING

Tom stared at the cage of trunks all around them in dismay. *How are we going to fight now?* A delighted peal of laughter echoed down into his prison from above. Tom looked up to see Ria leaning over the rail of her flying boat, peering down at him and Elenna. He clenched his jaw.

"Poor Tom!" Ria said. "You and

your little friend seem to have got yourselves stuck. Which is very convenient for me, because I have some slaves to punish for trying to escape. I expect I'll have to ask Jurog to dismember a few, to remind the rest who's boss." Ria grinned down at Tom, her green eyes full of glee. "Maybe you two should think about that while I leave you here to rot. After all, it is all your fault," she said. "Come on, Jurog." Ria beckoned to the Beast. Then she tipped Tom and Elenna a wave, and sailed her flying dinghy out of view.

Tom swallowed the fury rising in his chest. "We have to get out of here so we can help those people!"

"Well, there's no way we'll fit between those trunks," Elenna said. "Can you use your magical strength to knock one or two down?"

"Good idea," Tom said. He called on the strength of his golden breastplate, then leapt feet first at one of the giant trees. The impact sent him flying backwards. The tree trembled, and a few leaves fluttered down, but it didn't budge. *Let's try another tactic*, Tom thought. He wrapped his arms around a thick trunk, bent his knees and heaved upwards. The blood soon thundered in his skull as he strained every muscle... Nothing.

"The trunks are buried too deep!"

Tom growled, his body burning with rage and frustration. "There's no way to get out! Grr!" He focused to harness the power of his golden breastplate one more time, drawing back his fist and driving it hard into the nearest trunk. The wood splintered, leaving a deep dent in the trunk.

"Well, that seems to work quite well," Elenna said. Tom turned to her, grinning, suddenly feeling foolish and hopeful at the same time.

"Stand back," he said. Then he swung his fist over and over at the trunk. After six blows, he punched through to the other side, then

set about widening the hole, until
it was just big enough for them
to wiggle through. Elenna went
first, squirming easily through the

opening. Tom scrambled after her, the jagged wood snagging at his clothes, then tumbled out into the clearing.

Tom got to his feet, and drew his sword. "Follow as fast as you can," he told Elenna.

"Good luck!" Elenna called as Tom raced back through the jungle using the speed of his magical leg armour. He only slowed his pace when he reached the edge of the clearing where Ria worked her slaves. Despite his speed, he could already hear the pirate witch bellowing orders, as well as the booming thump of Jurog's footsteps.

"Tom!" a familiar voice called. Tom turned to see Daltec step out from behind a mossy rock. "I have a plan to defeat the Beast!" the wizard said. Daltec beckoned excitedly for Tom to follow him behind the rock, where Isaac crouched before an immense pile of metal chains.

"We sneaked into the clearing and gathered all the chains we could find before Ria could capture her workers again," Daltec said. "Unfortunately, with Ria's Beast still on the rampage, the workers were too afraid to flee. Although all her pirates seem to have vanished. Anyway, I used my magic to forge these chains together."

Tom ran his eyes over the huge pile of chains, and smiled. "I reckon

I know what you're thinking," he said. "Wait here for Elenna – I'm going to snare a Beast!"

Calling on the magical strength of his golden breastplate, Tom slung the mass of looped chain over his shoulder. With a free length gripped in one hand like a lasso, Tom strode out into the clearing. Jurog stood in the centre of the space, swinging his tail this way and that, sending it crashing down close to terrified workers. Ria stood tall in her dinghy high above, laughing as her slaves cowered in terror or ran for their lives.

"Pull a few legs off!" Ria called down to Jurog. "That'll keep them from running!" Jurog shrugged his huge shoulders then reached a giant hand towards a young woman pressed up against a pile of logs. The woman's knees gave way with horror and she covered her face with her hands.

It's now or never! Tom thought. Before the Beast could snatch the woman from where she cowered, Tom swung the length of chain in his hand and lashed it towards Jurog's legs. The chain wrapped twice around the monkey Beast's ankles. Jurog snarled, his head whipping round, eyes blazing with fury. Tom wrenched the chain hard, pulling it tight, making Jurog

stagger back from his prey. Then
Tom ran.

From above, Tom could hear Ria
shouting curses as he charged in
circles around the Beast, binding

the creature's legs tightly together. Huge fists swiped his way, but each blow missed as Tom sprinted on with magical speed, only stopping when he ran out of chain. Then with one mighty wrench, Tom tugged the end hard. Jurog let out a furious snarl and toppled, huge arms flailing as he crashed towards the ground with a mighty boom that sent tremors through the earth. The Beast twisted and snarled, trying to push himself upright. But as Tom watched, a surge of villagers rushed towards the Beast's fallen body, grabbing Jurog's arms and pinning them down.

Jurog's tail lashed back and forth,

striking blindly towards the people swarming his body. Suddenly one dark-haired slave leapt from the Beast's back, wielding a huge axe with both hands.

Isaac's father! Tom realised. Powerful muscles stood out on the man's lean arms as he drew back his axe, watching the writhing tail…

CHOP! Isaac's father hacked the spiked mace free. The Beast's hairy tail writhed harmlessly for a moment more, then blurred before Tom's eyes and vanished. The villagers on Jurog's body let out cries of surprise and alarm, jumping back from the Beast as the giant monkey's body faded into the dirt,

leaving just a pile of chain and a
spiked redsteel ball.

"You and your friends might have
spoiled my fun, Tom!" Ria called

from above. "But don't think you can stop me. You're nothing but a fly in a mug of grog. I'll spit you out!"

Anger coursed through Tom's veins. He let out a hoarse cry of rage and leapt. The power of his golden boots carried him high up over the clearing to land with a thud in Ria's boat. The vessel rocked wildly beneath his feet, then lurched forwards to soar over the jungle.

Ria's mouth opened in shock as she staggered to get her balance. Then her green eyes narrowed to angry slits. Her hands whipped out, closing around Tom's throat. Tom quickly returned the favour, placing his hands either side of Ria's neck. Red spots swam in his vision as Ria's grip tightened, but Tom knew his strength was greater...if only he could bring himself to use it!

Suddenly, Tom felt Ria's grip around his throat weaken. She let out a strange, breathy wheezing sound, tears leaking from her eyes. For a heartbeat, Tom thought she was really in trouble and loosened his grip. But then he gaped at her in disbelief. *She's laughing!*

"What's so funny?" Tom demanded, dropping his hands.

"You are!" Ria said. "It doesn't matter if you kill me, you see. My fleet is ready, and will attack regardless. Turn around, Tom. Take a look." She gestured out over the jungle, towards the glinting shoreline of the island. Tom turned and immediately felt as if as the breath been punched from his body.

So that's where Ria's pirates went...

All around the tip of the island, bobbing in the ocean and hanging in the air, floated rows and rows of square-rigged pirate ships, cannons poking from their hulls. A whole armada of magical vessels, ready to sail for Tom's homeland. He stared in dismay, his body bowed beneath the terrible weight of defeat. Sickness rose in his throat at the thought of all the people who would suffer...all

the people he had failed.

"Avantia will be razed to the ground," said Ria, "and there's nothing you and your pathetic friends can do to stop me."

But through the hopelessness in the pit of his stomach, Tom suddenly remembered Aduro's words on the day he'd set out on this Quest. *Four magical tokens*, the former wizard had said. *Four ancient Beasts. The final Beast must guard those ships!* Tom scanned the waiting vessels and balled his fists, determination swelling in his chest. *While there's blood in my veins*, Tom vowed, *not a single one of those ships will ever set sail for Avantia. Whatever it takes,*

I'll defeat that final Beast – and Ria and her pirates too. This is all or nothing now!

THE END

CONGRATULATIONS, YOU HAVE COMPLETED THIS QUEST!

At the end of each chapter you were awarded a special gold coin.
The QUEST in this book was worth an amazing 8 coins.

Look at the Beast Quest totem picture inside the back cover of this book to see how far you've come in your journey to become

MASTER OF THE BEASTS.

The more books you read, the more coins you will collect!

Do you want your own
Beast Quest Totem?

1. Cut out and collect the coin below
2. Go to the Beast Quest website
3. Download and print out your totem
4. Add your coin to the totem
www.beastquest.co.uk/totem

Don't miss the next exciting Beast Quest book, NERSEPHA, THE CURSED SIREN!
Read on for a sneak peek...

ARMADA

Tom gripped on tight to the gunwale, his gaze fixed on Ria. The pirate captain stood at the prow of the flying dinghy. The breeze ruffled her scarlet mohawk, and swayed the strands of the cat-o'-nine-tails which dangled from her right hand.

"It's over," she sneered. "You've failed."

Tom glanced over Ria's shoulder, feeling sick at the sight of the vast fleet of ships filling the distant bay. Some bobbed on the waves, moored just off the wide crescent of sandy

beach. Others clustered in the skies above, swarming like vultures, powered by the floating fuel Ria had mined from the Elixir Wells of Makai.

I was so sure I could stop her gathering a fleet, Tom thought. *But I*

was wrong.

He gritted his teeth. Ria had turned out to be an even deadlier foe than her parents, the witch Kensa and the pirate Sanpao. And if she were to bring her fleet to Avantia, there was no telling what destruction it would unleash.

Which is why I'm going to put an end to this, right now!

Drawing his sword, Tom leapt forward. But Ria was quicker. She swung her cat-o'-nine-tails and Tom ducked, feeling a sharp gust as the strands passed just above his head, crackling with blue electricity.

Ria laughed. "Do you understand how pointless your Quest has been?"

she crowed. "What can one boy do against the greatest fleet ever assembled? My mother and father might have failed, but I will achieve what they never could...I'll raid your homeland, Tom. Oh, and I can't wait to reach Errinel! Your aunt and uncle will make such excellent slaves..."

Hot anger surged through Tom. He lunged, his sword flashing, but Ria easily sidestepped, and Tom's blade whistled through nothing but air.

With a grunt, Ria brought her flail round hard, smacking it on to Tom's shield. The impact sent him stumbling, his shin hitting the edge of the dinghy. He overbalanced.

"Goodbye, Tom," snarled Ria.

Panic rising, Tom swung his arms, trying to recover. But Ria viciously lashed her cat-o'-nine-tails once again.

Szzzzzz! Tom's shoulder exploded with pain as the electrified strands

hit him. He clutched at the wound with his sword arm, but it was too late. He plummeted, dropping through the sky. As the treetops rushed towards him, he tried to lift his shield, hoping to use the magic of Arcta's feather to slow his fall – but his arm was dead, hanging limp and lifeless from Ria's blow.

He crashed through the uppermost leaves, then slammed into one branch that flipped him over as it cracked, then a second that knocked the wind from his stomach. Twigs lashed his face and snagged his clothes, before he struck the ground with a sickening *crack*. His ankle twisted, and he slumped on to the earth.

He lay listening to his own heavy breathing. His body throbbed with pain in a thousand places. *But I'm alive...just!*

"Tom!"

At the familiar voice, Tom rolled cautiously on to his side, wincing with the movement. Elenna was running through the trees with Daltec, the wizard's robes fluttering as he panted to keep up, holding on to his hat with one hand.

Elenna knelt at Tom's side. "Are you hurt?" she said.

Tom nodded. He unfastened the green jewel from his belt and held its cool surface against his ankle, drawing on its healing power. He felt a sharp burst of pain as a bone slid back into place. Then he flexed his foot. *Ouch! I'll be hobbling for a while...*

"Where's Ria?" asked Daltec.

Tom shook his head as he replaced the green jewel. "Sorry, she..." He grunted – it was an effort to speak. "She got away."

As Elenna helped him up into a sitting position, Tom saw more figures appearing through the trees. He recognised some of them – they were the villagers that Ria had enslaved to cut timber for her ships. Many of them still had iron cuffs and chains trailing from their wrists and ankles, but Tom saw one older villager going among them with a key, releasing them one by one.

A young boy with a mop of black hair rushed up to Tom, a slingshot poking out from his belt. It was

Isaac, the boy whose life Tom had saved in his battle with Jurog. Isaac stared at Tom's wounded shoulder with wide eyes. Tom realised that his tunic was ripped and the skin scorched black by the flail. "Did Ria do that?" asked Isaac.

Tom nodded. "I'm sorry I couldn't stop her."

"You saved us all, Tom of Avantia," said a man with matching black hair, laying a hand on Isaac's shoulder. "You have nothing to apologise for."

Read
NERSEPHA THE CURSED SIREN
to find out what happens next!

Fight the Beasts,
Fear the Magic

Do you want to know more
about BEAST QUEST?
Then join our Quest Club!

Visit
www.beastquest.co.uk/club
and sign up today!

Are you a collector of the Beast Quest Cards?
Visit the website for further information.

Beast Quest

OUT NOW!

The epic adventure is brought to life on **Xbox One** and **PS4** for the first time ever!

www.maximumgames.com   www.beast-quest.com